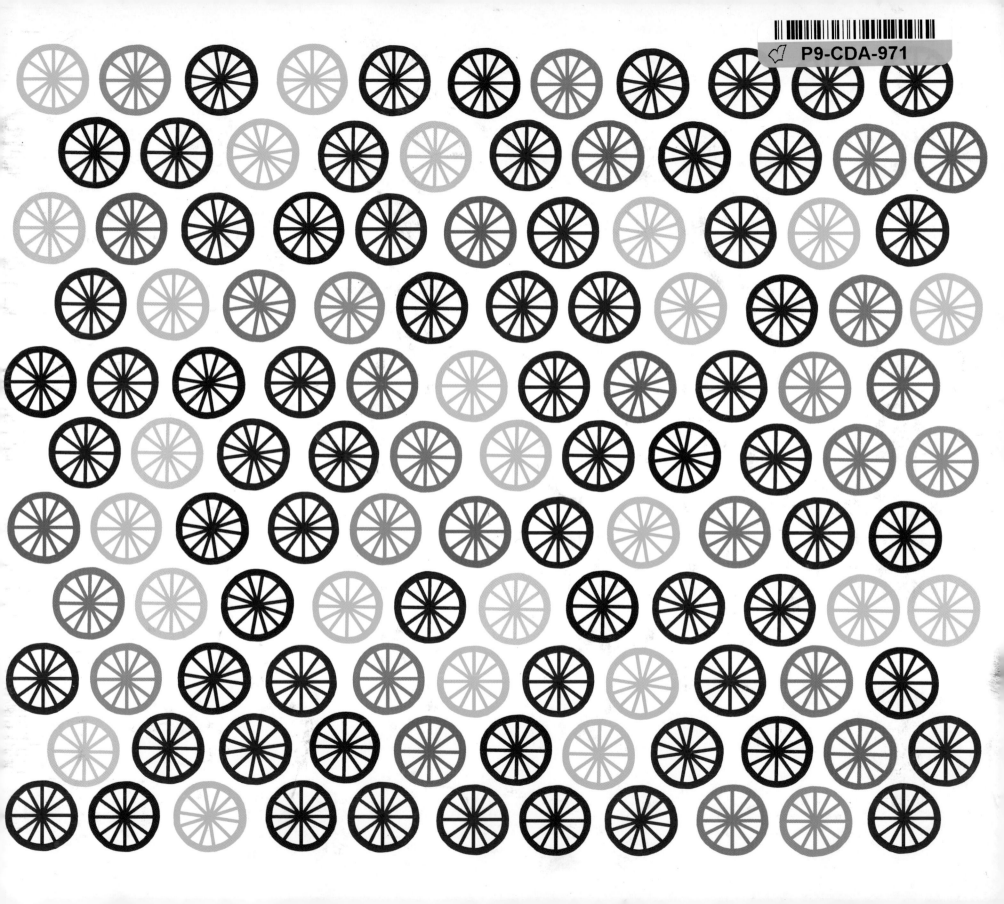

With thanks to my two guinea pigs . . .
Aidan and **Beau**

First U.S. edition 2007

Library of Congress Cataloging-in-Publication Data is available.

Library of Congress Catalog Card Number 2006043857

ISBN 978-0-7636-3248-9

10 9 8 7 6 5 4 3 2 1

Printed in China

This book was typeset in Frutiger.
The illustrations were done in pen, ink, and Macintosh.

Candlewick Press
2067 Massachusetts Avenue
Cambridge, Massachusetts 02140

visit us at www.candlewick.com

and the train goes...

william bee

CANDLEWICK PRESS
CAMBRIDGE, MASSACHUSETTS

Here is the station all noisy and full,
and the station clock goes,
Tick-tock, tickerty-tock . . .

and the man in the station office cries,
"Hurry up! Hurry up! Any more tickets . . . ?"

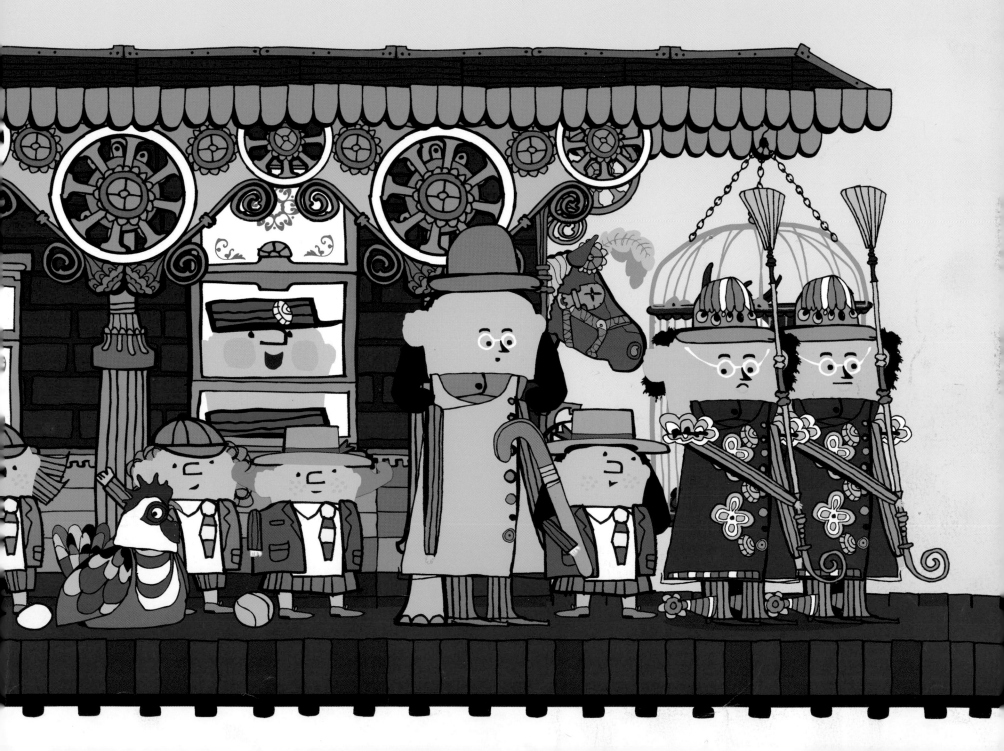

Here is the train all ready to go,
and the station master calls out,
"All aboard who are coming aboard . . ."

Here is the train leaving the station,
and its whistle blows:

Woo-woo, woo-woo . . .

Here is the fireman shoveling coal,
and he mutters,
"Shovel-shovel, shovel-shovel . . ."

and the train goes,
Chuff-chuff, chufferty-chuff . . .

Here are the ladies off to the races,
and they chitter and chatter:
"Lovely cake, Doris. Lovely tea, Mabel . . ."

and the train goes,
Puff-puff, pufferty-puff . . .

Here are the soldiers off on parade,
and their sergeant major bellows,
"Left, right, left, right . . . at ease . . ."

and the train goes,
**Clickerty-click, clickerty-clack,
clickerty-click, clickerty-clack . . .**

Here is the school class off on a trip,
and the children yell,
"Please, sir, please, ma'am . . . are we there yet?"

and the train goes,
Clickerty-click, clickerty-clack . . .

Here are the businessmen off to the city,
and they shout,
"Faster, faster! Time is money, time is money . . ."

and the train goes,
**Clickerty-click, clickerty-clack,
clickerty-click, clickerty-clack . . .**

Here are the chickens off to the market,
and they go,
Cluck-cluck, cluckerty-cluck . . .

and the train goes,
**Clickerty-click, clickerty-clack,
clickerty-click, clickerty-clack . . .**

Here is the guard . . . asleep on the job . . .
and he goes . . .
Snore-snore, snore-snore, snore . . .

and the train goes,
Clickerty-click, clickerty-clack,
woo-wooooo!

And here is the station all quiet and empty,
and the station clock goes,
Tick-tock, tickerty-tock . . .

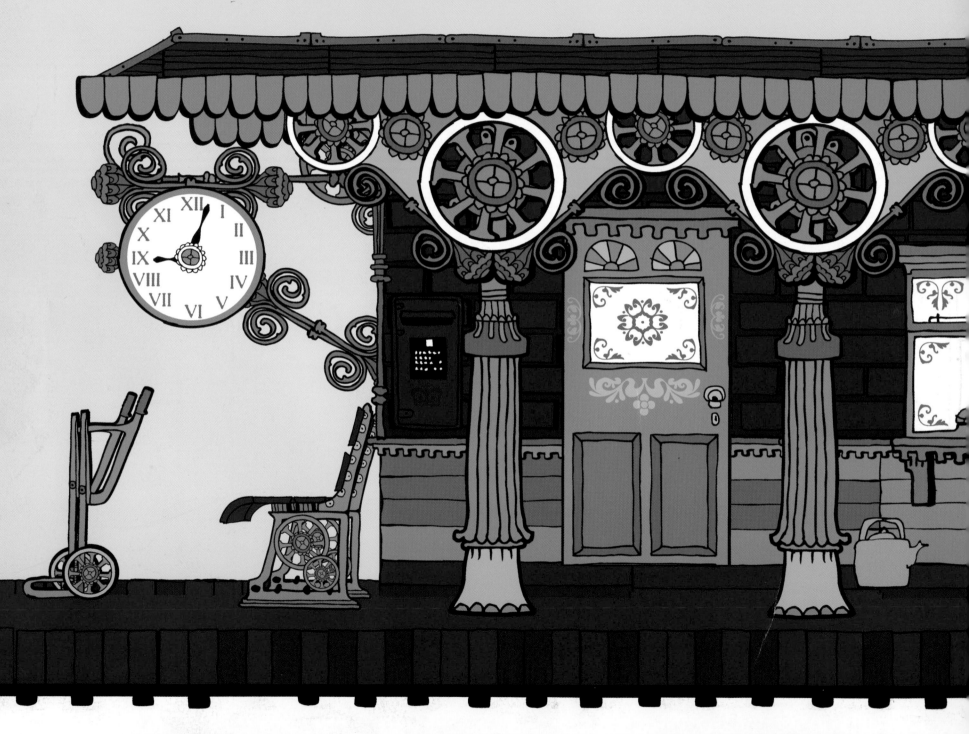

And here is the station parrot,
and he goes . . .

"Hurry up! Hurry up!
All aboard! All aboard!
Shovel-shovel, shovel-shovel,
Chuff-chuff, chufferty-chuff,
Lovely cake, lovely cake,
Left, right, left, right, at ease . . .
Please, sir, please, ma'am,
Time is money, time is money!
Cluck-cluck, cluckerty-cluck,
Clickerty-click, clickerty-clack,
Squawk-squawk, squawkerty-squawk,
Woo-woooooooooooooooooooooooo . . ."

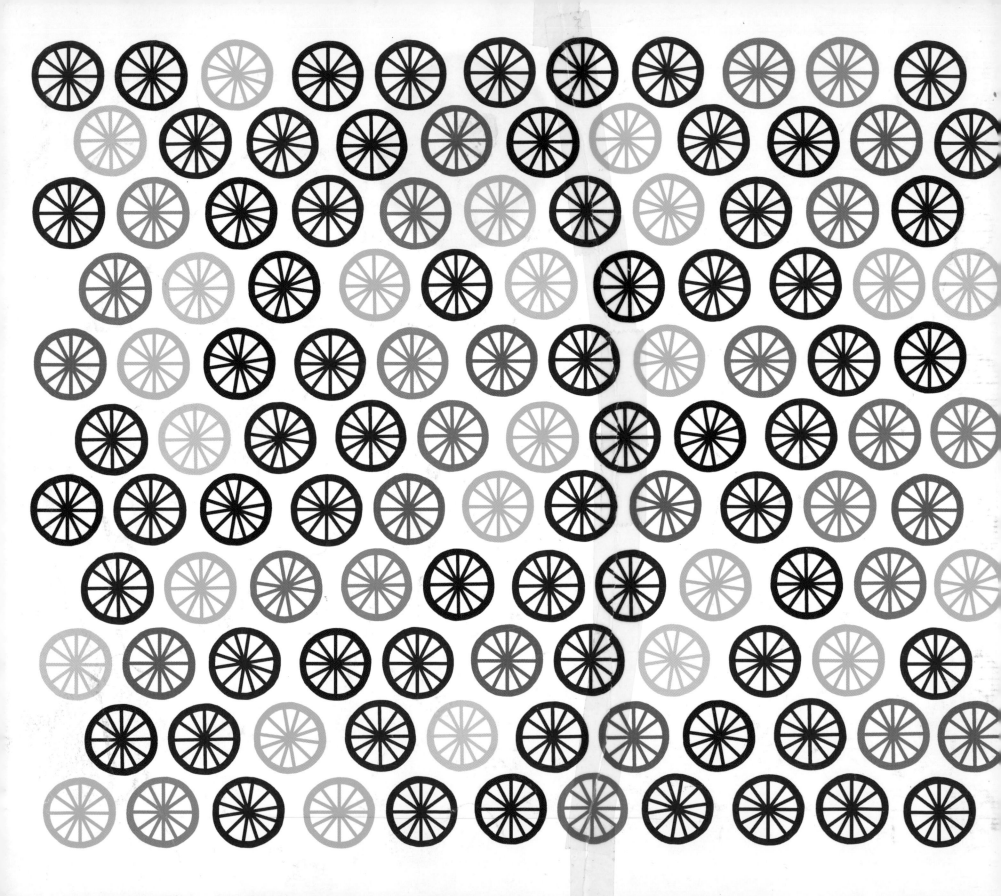